Jane wished she had long red hair, thick and waving, down to her waist, and that her mother would let her wear it loose every day, not just for parties...that her name was Amanda or Melissa, or at least Elizabeth...that she was an only child....

But Jane's wishes inevitably crumble in the face of her family's practical, down-to-earth view of things: "Red hair doesn't run in our family"; "I like 'Jane'. What's wrong with 'Jane'?" "I remember when I was little, I was an only child and I would have been happy to have a big sister I could share everything with...."

Told almost entirely in dialogue, this delightful story of a dreamy little girl and her wide-awake but not unsympathetic family will draw a rueful smile of recognition from all wishful thinkers.

Tobi Tobias and Trina Schart Hyman wrote and illustrated *The Quitting Deal*, recently published by Viking. Here again they have combined words and pictures to produce a warm, contemporary picture book.

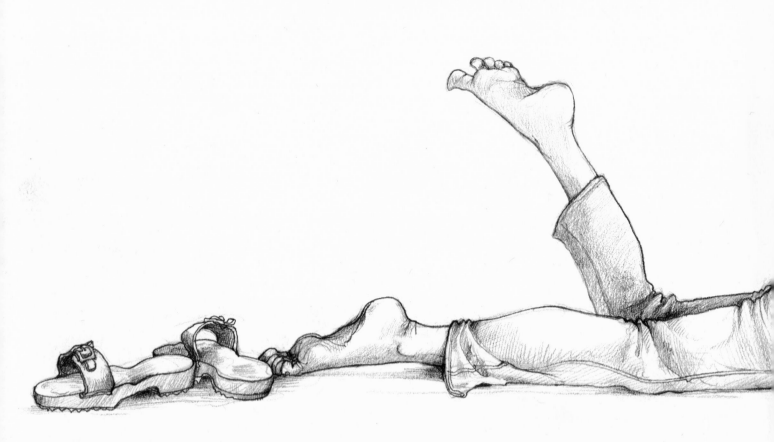

JANE, WISHING

TOBI TOBIAS

pictures by trina schart hyman

THE VIKING PRESS   NEW YORK

for my mother

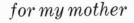

First Edition
Text Copyright © Tobi Tobias, 1977
Illustrations Copyright © Trina Schart Hyman, 1977
All rights reserved
First published in 1977 by The Viking Press
625 Madison Avenue, New York, N.Y. 10022
Published simultaneously in Canada by
The Macmillan Company of Canada Limited
Printed in U.S.A.

1 2 3 4 5 81 80 79 78 77

Library of Congress Cataloging in Publication Data
Tobias, Tobi.   Jane, Wishing.
[1. Wishes—Fiction. 2. Self-perception—Fiction]
I. Hyman, Trina Schart. II. Title. PZ7.T56Jan [E] 76–27673

ISBN 0–670–40565–5

Jane wished she had long red hair, thick and waving,
down to her waist, and that her mother would let her
wear it loose every day, not just for parties.

Braids for school, loose for special occasions.

Red hair doesn't run in our family.

Personally I like blond hair the best. Especially when it's curly. Sort of like mine.

Who cares about dumb hair?

Jane, it's shampoo time and please make sure you brush your hair very well first so it doesn't come out all tangles. You know what it felt like last time, combing out those wet knots.

She wished she had sea-green sea-blue eyes that changed according to the weather or the color of her dress.

You have nice brown eyes, like your Daddy. What's wrong with brown eyes?

I have blue eyes. Grandma said she likes blue best.

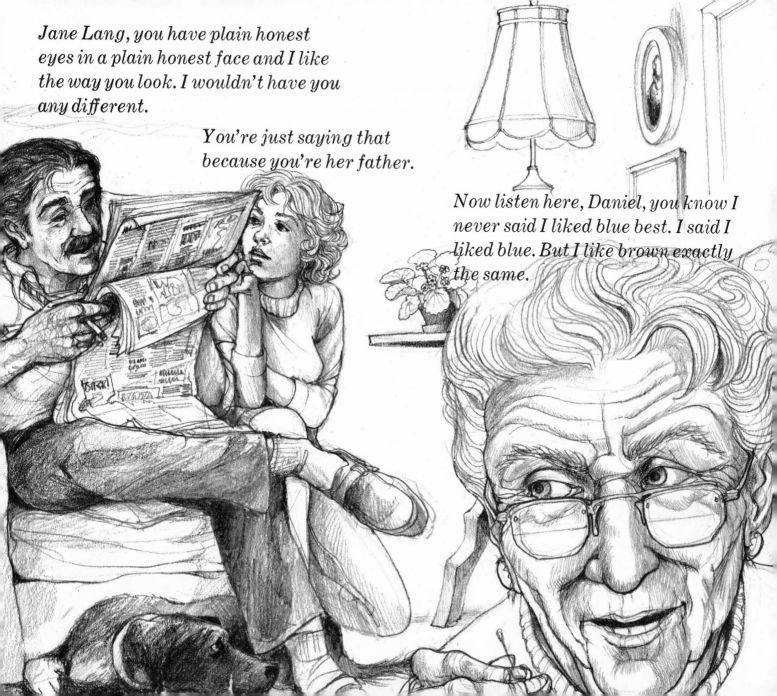

Jane Lang, you have plain honest eyes in a plain honest face and I like the way you look. I wouldn't have you any different.

You're just saying that because you're her father.

Now listen here, Daniel, you know I never said I liked blue best. I said I liked blue. But I like brown exactly the same.

She wished she had pale skin that you could almost
see through, like Melissa Grant's down the block,
and that her cheeks would flush pink when she was
excited, the way princesses' do, in stories.

I remember the first time your grandfather saw me. He said, Elizabeth Jane West, you look like a storybook princess, come to life.

You don't still read those dopey fairy tales, do you?

She wished her name was Amanda or Melissa, or at least Elizabeth.

She wished she could sing with the kind of voice that makes people look at each other and say, "That child has a natural talent."

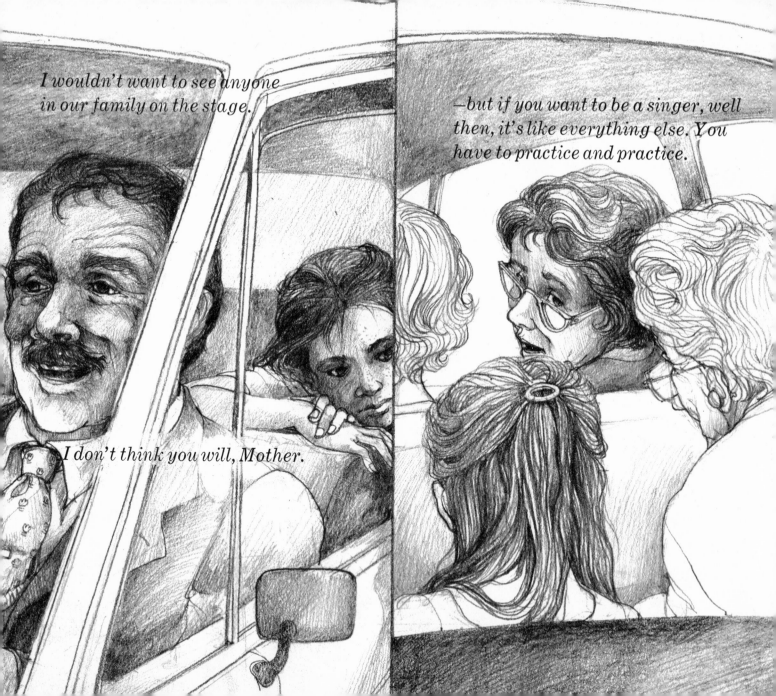

She wished she had the kind of smile that made people want to do things for her.

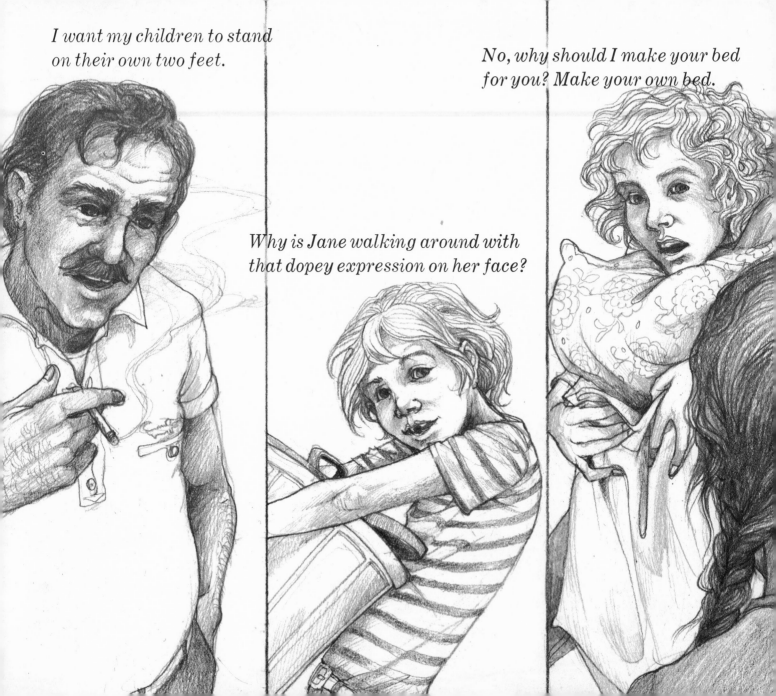

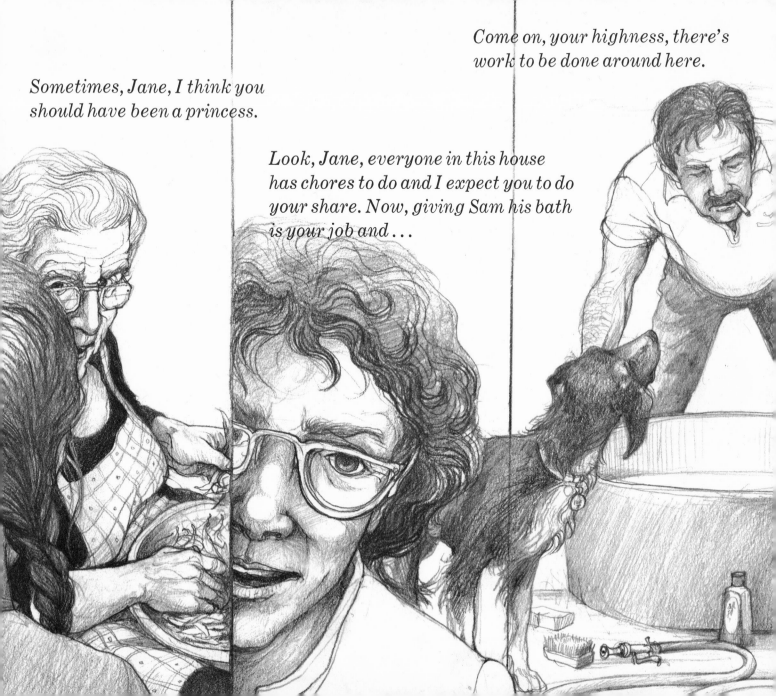

She wished she had a silky black kitten all her own instead of sharing a mixed-up, every-kind-of dog with Margaret and Daniel.

She would call that kitten "Night."

Jane, honey, what we DON'T *need here is a cat. First of all, your sister's allergic to them. You remember how they make her start sneezing and wheezing and crying—*

Now look, Jane, you know that giving Sam his bath is your job and—

Which part of Sam is my part?

You're hurting his feelings

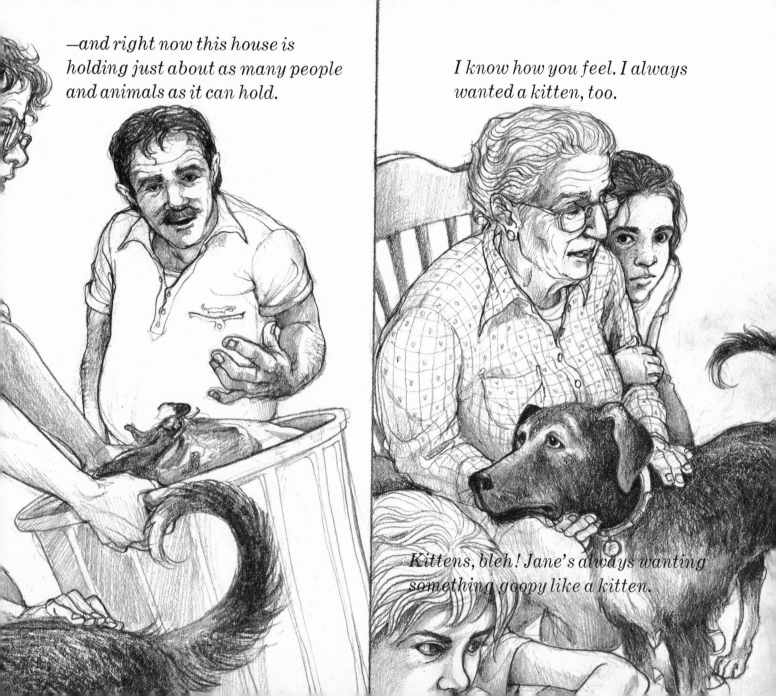

She wished she were an only child.

I like a good-sized family.
It feels like home.

Oh how I dreamed of having a sister.
It would be like having your best
friend come to stay over, forever.

She wished Kate Jordan would be her best friend.

What's so special about Kate Jordan?
Do you mean that dark, quiet one?
Does she ever talk?

Kate Jordan, ugh. She's even
worse that that icky, stuck-up
Melissa Grant.

I know what you mean.

Jane, dear, maybe she's shy. Why don't you invite her here to play one afternoon? Now, don't say she wouldn't come. You never know until you try. Someone's got to do the asking first.

Jordan? Jordan? I used to know some people in that family. They think a lot of themselves. Why I remember one time when Tom Jordan—he must be Kate's father...

I still don't see what's so special about Kate Jordan.

I do.

She wished she had a room of her own, with everything beautiful in it . . .

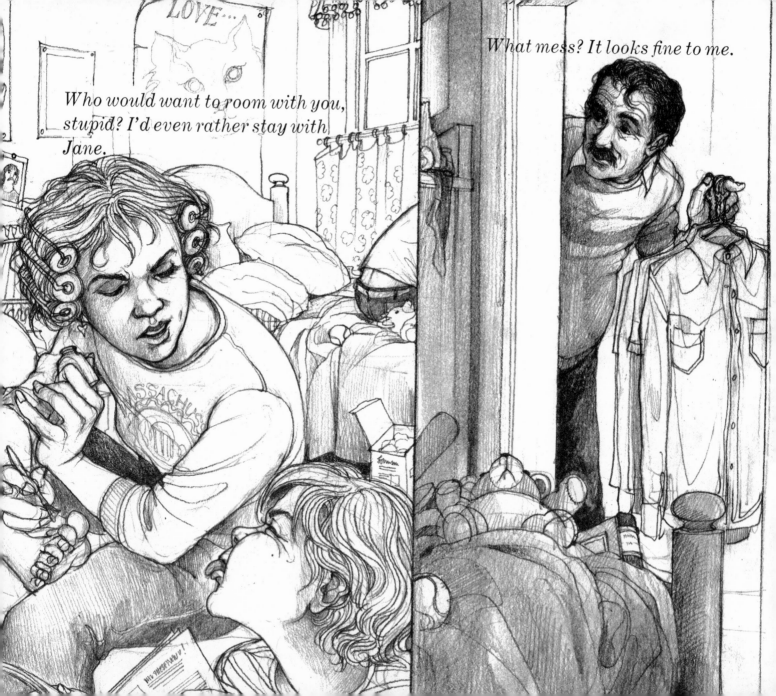

... where she could look out a big round window and wish, secretly, on the night stars, and make all her wishes come true.

Jane, are you still mooning at that window? I want you to stop dreaming and come down here and get that homework done. Right now.

I used to dream a lot when I was your age, but you must remember, Jane, nothing ever comes of it.

You can't see anything out that window but the McCloskey yard.

I saw the first star first, so it's MY wish.

But she didn't.

So she decided to be happy anyway.

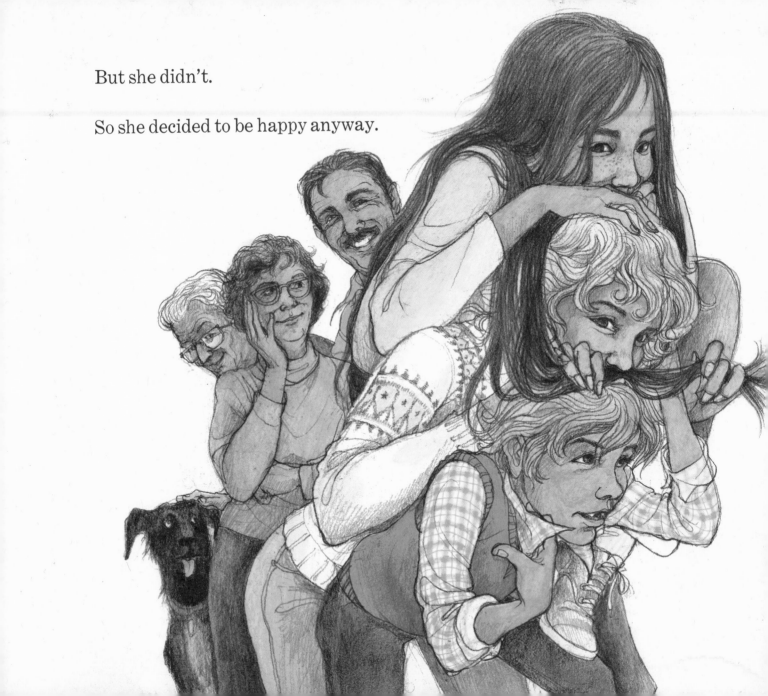